To Heidi and Fritz

Text and illustrations © 2013 Christoph Niemann

Published in North America in 2015 by Owlkids Books Inc.

Originally published as *Der Kartoffelkönig* in 2013 by Verlagshaus Jacoby & Stuart

Owlkids Books acknowledges the financial support of the Canada Council for the Arts, the Ontario Arts Council, the Government of Canada through the Canada Book Fund (CBF) and the Government of Ontario through the Ontario Media Development Corporation's Book Initiative for our publishing activities.

Published in Canada by
Owlkids Books Inc.
10 Lower Spadina Avenue
Toronto, ON M5V 2Z2

Published in the United States by
Owlkids Books Inc.
1700 Fourth Street
Berkeley, CA 94710

Library and Archives Canada Cataloguing in Publication

Niemann, Christoph [Kartoffelkönig. English]
    The potato king / written and illustrated by Christoph Niemann.

Translation of: Der kartoffelkönig.
ISBN 978-1-77147-139-8 (bound)

    1. Frederick II, King of Prussia, 1712-1786--Juvenile fiction. I. Title. II. Title: Kartoffelkönig. English.

PZ7.N59Po 2015   j833'.92   C2014-906142-0

Library of Congress Control Number: 2014950139

Manufactured in Shenzhen, Guangdong, China, in October 2014, by WKT Co. Ltd.
Job #14CB1340

A   B   C   D   E   F

 Publisher of Chirp, chickaDEE and OWL
www.owlkidsbooks.com

The Potato King

Christoph Niemann

Owlkids Books

There was once a king called Fritz.
One day he heard about a new wonder plant
from South America: the potato.

He planted a big field in a nearby village.
And he spoke to his citizens:

"Hear, hear! I give you the potato.
It costs little to grow and
is healthy to boot!"

The people, however,

didn't like to be told
what to eat.

King Fritz was upset.

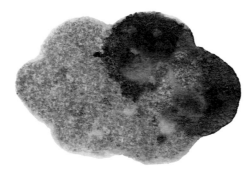

Then he had an idea.

He ordered his soldiers to
march to the village…

...and guard the potato field.

"Hmm…"
thought the villagers.

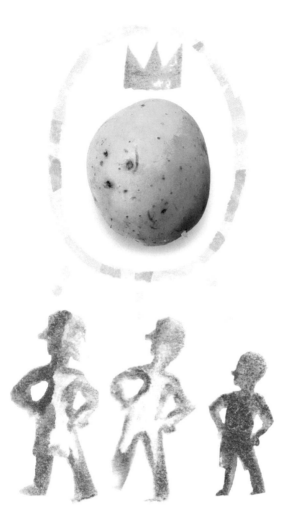

"If a vegetable has to be so
closely guarded, there must
be something special about it."

The king had ordered the guards

to go easy on their watch at night...

...baiting the locals to steal the crop

for their own gardens.

The potato flourished and
has lived on as a key ingredient in
local kitchens ever since.

This story may be a myth.

But to this day, people honor
King Fritz by putting potatoes
on his grave.

A Brief History of the Potato

The potato was first farmed thousands of years ago in South America. Although the leaves of the potato plant are poisonous, its swollen underground stem—called a *tuber*—is both tasty and healthful. The potato was one of the staple crops of the Inca empire, farmed alongside quinoa (say: KEEN-wah) and corn.

The plant was first brought to Europe by Spanish explorers. They had traveled to South America in search of gold but returned with potatoes instead. Sailors realized that the tubers were a good food supply to store onboard their ships. But the potato did not become popular in Europe until the late 1700s.

King Frederick the Great of Prussia (also known as Fritz) believed that the potato could help feed his nation. But his people did not trust this strange new plant. In 1774, Frederick issued an order for his subjects to grow potatoes to protect against famine. But the people of the town of Kolberg replied: "The things have neither smell nor taste, not even the dogs will eat them, so what use are they to us?"

According to legend, Frederick decided to try a bit of trickery. He planted a royal field of potatoes and sent guards to protect the crop from thieves. The local peasants became curious. Surely anything worth guarding was worth stealing. At night, they snuck into the royal field and snatched the plants to grow at home. Of course, this was exactly what Frederick had wanted.

Today, potatoes are one of the most popular foods around the world. After corn, wheat, and rice, this once-mistrusted plant is now the fourth-largest food crop on Earth.